SPOOKY
Back Pocket B

Written and Illustrated by
Jon and Di Nelson

Spooky Stuff – Back Pocket Bonfire Tales

ISBN: 9798745245572

spookystuffbook.com

Follow the scream guide,
and enjoy the ride!

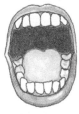 The more screams,
the spookier the story...

CONTENTS

SPOOKY STUFF

"Time for a story," Nana says.

"Is it a scary one?" we ask.

"It is," Nana replies.

"Hooray!" we scream.

Swamp Island Camp

It was getting hard to find a camp where Nora Fisher was still welcome. She had been kicked out of every summer camp in the Kawarthas, and even the camps north of there had heard the stories.

She wasn't a bad kid, she just did bad things sometimes. She didn't like how her parents were always sending her and her little brother, Ollie, away for the summer. They cared too much about their jobs, and not enough about family time.

The school year was almost over and her parents still hadn't found a spot. Ms Fisher was desperately calling friends and relatives for suggestions, hoping somebody might just offer to babysit for a while. Finally she called Nora's great grandmother.

"Well, when I was a little girl, I used to spend each summer at Swamp Island Camp in the middle of Algonquin Park. It was actually quite lovely despite the name. The camp itself was barebones, but boy did I learn a thing or two there. I would give an arm and a leg to spend another summer on Swamp Island. Happiest times I can remember. You know, that's where I met Bob. The love of my life."

"Okay I'm looking up Swamp Island Camp here, but I'm not seeing anything online. Do you have an address? Or a phone number?"

There was a pause.

"Florence?"

"Oh yes, I'm just checking my Rolodex dear. Here it is. Ray Gatecliff is the guy to call."

Ms Fisher was quite sure that Ray was no longer the "guy to call" but she was running out of options so she gave it a try. Somebody picked up the phone. The line was a bit crackly but she could hear a very peppy man saying "Top of the morning! It's a swell day here at Swamp Island Camp in the Algonquin Highlands. Come check it out for yourself. It'll flip your lid!"

"Ummm...hello? Is this a recording?"

"What's your story, morning glory? Are you hoping to send your little ones to camp this summer?"

"Oh. Yes I am. You're open? Do you still have space?"

"Yes ma'am we do. New campers sure would be exciting. The same kids keep coming year after year. Once a Swamper, always a Swamper, I guess."

They continued their strange conversation, and by the end of it Nora and Ollie were both signed up to spend the entire summer away at Swamp Island Camp.

The list of items looked like it hadn't been updated in a while.

Swimming costume
Bedroll
Rucksack
Union suits
Supportive footwear

Ms Fisher found it all very charming and old-fashioned, but Nora and Ollie weren't thrilled. They had been to a lot of camps, and this one sounded way more rustic than any of the others.

Summer arrived and the car was packed with two giant duffel bags. The whole family was along for the ride. When they reached Algonquin Park, their GPS lost its signal and Mr Fisher pulled out the handwritten directions that Florence had sent them in the mail.

"Okay kids...we're looking for a big mossy rock on the right hand side of the road."

"Are you kidding me?" asked Nora. "This place is covered in mossy rocks."

"Well, it says here that we'll know it when we see it. It looks like a giant's head."

And sure enough, a gigantic mossy rock with hollows that looked like eyes, appeared on the right hand side.

They turned onto an overgrown road littered with fallen branches and tall grass that brushed the underside of the

vehicle. After kilometres of bumpy terrain, the trees parted
and they found themselves at the edge of a sparkling lake.
There was nothing in sight but a rickety, waterlogged dock.
Nora and Ollie reluctantly dragged their belongings out of the
trunk.

In the distance, a rowboat appeared. As it got closer, the
Fishers all exchanged looks, confused.

"Do you guys see anybody in that boat?" Ollie asked.
They stood in silence, squinting their eyes, trying to figure
out how it was moving. Suddenly, as if out of thin air, a man
in an old orange life jacket appeared behind the oars, whis-
tling as he rowed. The tin boat brushed alongside the dock

and with little effort, the man tied up.

"Howdy Fisher family! Ollie? Nora? I'm Ray. But people around here call me Raven. We go by nature names at Swamp Island. So you can think about your new names on the trip back to camp. They should tell us something about your personalities."

Ms Fisher was embarrassed when Nora rolled her eyes, but Ray didn't seem to notice.

"You're both going to have a swell time, I guarantee ya!"

"Thank you, Ray," said Ms Fisher with a bit of hesitancy. "So...it's just you doing the pickup? You don't have a motor boat coming or anything?"

"Oh golly no," he replied. "We're not like those other fancy pants camps. We believe in hard work and wilderness survival skills."

"I can get behind that!" said Mr Fisher. "Say, Ray... When you were paddling over here we all could've sworn there was nobody in your boat. It was the weirdest thing. But if I know the mind of a camp counsellor... I bet you were pulling some kind of prank on us, weren't ya!"

"Dad!" Ollie said.

"Back when I was a counsellor, son, we'd fill up a bowl with warm water, and..."

"Mike!" Ms Fisher interrupted.

"Hmmm," said Ray. "We don't stand for pranks at Swamp Island. But you know, a lot of people say this lake plays tricks on their eyes. Something about the way the sun reflects off the water. It's all a bunch of hullabaloo, but it makes for a good ghost story around the campfire."

Mr Fisher seemed satisfied with that answer. Ollie gave his parents a nervous glance. Nora gave them a wide-eyed stare, as if to say, *Are you actually going to send us off into the woods with this stranger?!*

Their parents looked at each other for a moment before Mr Fisher said, "Okay you two, have a great time at camp! We'll miss you a ton." And that was that.

The kids climbed into the rowboat and Ray started rowing. He paused, looked at Nora and Ollie, and made an "ahem" sound as he glanced toward the second set of oars. Nora gave her parents one last desperate look and when she realized they weren't going to save her, she grabbed an oar. Ollie followed. They had no idea what they were doing, but after some awkward splashing and encouragement from Ray, they caught on.

Ray turned out to be a pretty great guy. He lightened the mood in the rowboat with a bunch of goofy jokes, and he seemed to genuinely want to get to know both of the kids. Nora was trying to act unimpressed, but Ollie could tell she liked him too.

When they pulled up to Swamp Island Camp, the head counsellor, Fern, was waiting to bring them to their cabins. She was a short, muscular woman who looked like she could arm-wrestle a moose. As they walked through the grounds together, Nora and Ollie were awestruck.

This was unlike any camp they had ever been to. There were no buildings. The kitchen and dining area were outside. The "cabins" were just canvas tents. And there was no electricity.

Fern showed them to their bunks, and told them to get into their swimming costumes because everyone was at the beach. Nora asked for the closest washroom and Fern pointed to the forest.

"You'll find the thunder boxes behind those bushes."

"Sorry? Thunder boxes?" Nora asked.

Fern just nodded.

When Nora got back behind the bushes she saw a row of

four big wooden boxes with holes in the top. Judging by the smell, these were the "washrooms". She was shocked, but she also started giggling. Was this place for real? Was she about to spend an entire summer in the middle of nowhere with nothing but a box to pee in?

Everything that happened in their first week of camp surprised them. Swamp Island was so strange. Even the people were different. The kids were the same age as them, but they weren't like the kids back home. They seemed more mature, but also kind of innocent. Nobody swore or gossiped or complained about the backbreaking work they were sometimes asked to do.

Nora stopped looking over her shoulder for the mean girls. There were always mean girls at camp, and Nora could never resist giving them a taste of their own medicine. But at Swamp Island, everyone just drifted along in peaceful harmony. Ollie kept waiting for his sister to start pulling some of her troublemaker tricks, but a week went by and she hadn't been kicked out. He was relieved.

Nora picked Narwhal as her nature name. Narwhals swim in Arctic waters. Since Nora always made a point to be the first one to swim in the lake each spring, she thought it was a good fit. Ollie didn't think quite so hard about his nature name. He picked Otter because he thought otters were cool.

The siblings were starting to get used to Swamp Island in the daytime. But nighttime was a different story. Without electricity, they relied on the moon and their lanterns to see. And they had both seen *things*. Weird, unnatural things that made their flesh creep.

Ollie had a scare at the thunder boxes late one evening. He

could see a kid sitting on the far right box, so he sat down on the far left. As he finished his business and stood up to leave, he noticed that the kid was gone. Vanished. He hadn't heard a single footstep or rustling leaf. Spooky!

Nora had a similar experience in her tent. There was one spare bunk, where nobody slept. She woke up in the night to see a pale-faced girl sitting there, staring at her. She was so startled that she hid inside her sleeping bag, frozen in fear until the sun came up. When she found the courage to peek out, there was no sign of the girl.

Despite the uneasy feelings, Nora and Ollie didn't want to leave. Ollie had become good friends with another kid, Bobcat, who was pushing him to learn new skills like whittling wood, cooking with plants from the forest, and building shelters. He had a gentle way about him and a subtle sense of humour. Ollie felt like he had known Bobcat forever.

And since Nora wasn't looking for trouble like she usually did at camp, she was getting along with all the girls in her group. She liked that she was given real responsibilities. Fern trusted her to do things like chopping wood and building fires. She wasn't being treated like a little kid.

Before they knew it, a month had gone by and they hadn't thought twice about what they were missing in the city. Their great grandmother was right. Swamp Island Camp was the best.

Early one morning, Nora caught sight of something in the mist. A young girl was paddling all alone. How peaceful it was to sit on the end of the dock and watch her cedar strip canoe dance in circles without a ripple or a splash.

As the sun peeked over the horizon, the girl pulled her canoe up onto the beach and waved at Nora.

"Hi. It's nice to meet another early riser. Isn't dawn the

best time of day?" She held out her hand. One finger sparkled with an emerald ring.

"Woah, that's a beautiful ring," said Nora.

"Isn't it neat?" the girl replied. "It's a family heirloom. My name's Flower," she told Nora.

"I'm Narwhal."

"Oh! I love that! Narwhals are so unique with those huge tusks. The name suits you."

They were instant pals. Nora had never met anyone as carefree as Flower. She floated around camp, laughing and dancing and chatting with every kind of person. Not self-conscious like her friends at school, who always worried about their hair and their clothes. Nora decided to be more like Flower when she got back home.

Saturday nights were Swamp Gatherings. That's when Raven and Fern gave awards to acknowledge the campers' accomplishments. Nora was proud when Ollie received a cheer for most hardworking camper. He excelled at meal prep and clean-up. Who could have guessed? Her brother had never washed a pot in his life until this summer! Nora got recognized for her impressive fire keeper skills, never using more than one match to light a fire.

As the days got shorter, signalling the end of August, everyone sadly realized that camp was coming to an end. With heavy hearts the campers exchanged mailing addresses, and promised to keep in touch.

Nora and Ollie climbed into Raven's rowboat with their bags on the final day of camp. He didn't have to ask them to help. They pulled the oars with their strong, tanned arms, and watched as campers and counsellors gathered on the shore, waving and calling, "Goodbye, Narwhal! Goodbye, Otter! See you next summer!"

Their parents stood at the edge of the water at the north end of the lake, wondering who these capable young campers were. It was already clear that the summer had changed their kids for the better. The sullen-faced brats they had dropped off in July were gone. Replaced by kids who met them with happy smiles and warm embraces.

Everyone waved goodbye to Ray and piled into the car for the long journey home.

After the kids finished telling stories about their summer, they asked if they could go visit their great grandmother. They wanted to talk to a fellow Swamper.

Ms Fisher paused, and said, "We have some bad news about Florence. Your great grandmother passed away at the end of July. I'm so sorry kids. She died peacefully in her sleep. You know, she was 98 years old."

Nora and Ollie were quiet for the rest of the trip. They would never get a chance to talk to their great grandmother about Swamp Island Camp.

When they walked inside, the familiar smell of their family home wrapped around them like a warm quilt. Nora and Ollie missed camp already, but it was nice to be back. Their parents had left out an old photo album from Florence's camp days. The black and white picture on the front cover showed an old canvas tent. The swimming area and fire pit could be seen in the background. The kids were amazed.

"It hasn't changed one bit! Look, even the same canoes!"

They opened the cover and looked at the faded, grainy photographs that were eerily familiar. Ollie pointed to the campers and staff, standing at the edge of the lake.

"Does that look like Raven, Narwhal? I mean Nora?" It would take awhile to get out of the habit of calling each other by their nature names.

"It IS Raven, Ollie. That hat with the fishing lures!"

"But it couldn't be him. This photograph was taken, like, eighty years ago."

"Maybe it's Raven's grandfather."

"Or great grandfather?"

They turned the page. There was a young girl posing with her paddle. Ollie and Nora looked at each other and whispered the same word at the same time. "Flower..."

Page after page in the photo album revealed images of their fellow campers and counsellors. They were in shock.

Mr Fisher was pleased to see his two children so enthralled with the photo album. The summer had been good for them.

"By the way, Nora," he said. "Your great grandmother wanted you to have this." He handed Nora a small velvet box. In her heart, she knew what it was. She paused. Looked at Ollie.

"You open it," she said. "Please?"

When her brother pulled back the lid, a little emerald ring glittered and winked in the light.

The Great Chili Cook-Off

The Vermeers were hoping for a fresh start. Their hardware shop went under after a big box store took all their business. The only place they could find work was in a little town called Eerie Creek.

As they drove down the old-timey main street, with all their belongings towing behind, Nolan and Sienna finally stopped pouting. It looked like a real hometown. The siblings gazed, wide-eyed, at a bakeshop and a toy store, and a market with colourful fruits and vegetables displayed right on the sidewalk!

They had spent months complaining to their parents. Not wanting to move was the *only* thing those two could agree on. But maybe Eerie Creek wasn't going to be so bad after all.

Mrs Vermeer slowed the car as they drove down Oak Street, past a towering iron gate. A rusty fence wrapped around an overgrown property. Nolan rolled down the window to get a better look at the mansion, almost hidden by scraggly bushes and drooping vines.

"Our new house," he joked to Sienna.

"I hope not," she said. "It's creepy."

"Don't make judgments," Mrs Vermeer warned as she pulled into the driveway just past the mansion. "It's important to stay on good terms with our next door neighbours."

The whole family fell in love with Eerie Creek right away. Everyone in town was so welcoming. The only person they hadn't gotten to know was Mrs Fitz, next door, a quiet woman who lived alone with only her cats for company. Sienna was dangerously curious and desperately wanted to meet her. One day, the mail carrier noticed Sienna peeking through the bars of the giant gates.

"Have you met Mrs Fitz, yet?"

"No," Sienna said. "I keep trying to, but the gate's always locked and she never seems to come outside."

"I'm not surprised. Don't take it personally. Bobby-Jo keeps to herself. You know, she's a local success story."

"Seriously?"

"Yep. Her family was really poor, and she grew up in an old shack by the river. Her parents were hated by the rest of the town and ridiculed for being "lazy" and "trashy". But Bobby-Jo Fitz didn't let that stop her from making something of herself. She learned to cook delicious food and started selling it at the farmers' market and the church bazaar. You'll have to try it! One bite of Bobby-Jo's Nightmare Chili and there's no going back."

"Nightmare Chili?"

"That's what she calls it. It can keep you awake at night if you eat too much. It's a little on the spicy side. But take my word for it. After you taste it, you'll never be satisfied with ordinary chili again."

"Where can I buy some?"

"You'll have to wait for the Great Chili Cook-Off."

The Vermeers listened attentively at the dinner table that night as Sienna gave her report about Mrs Bobby-Jo Fitz.

"How lucky we are to have such a resilient neighbour!" Mrs Vermeer said. "She must be very busy with her business. Perhaps that's why we never catch a glimpse of her."

"Perhaps that's why she has no time to cut her grass or trim those scraggly lilac bushes," Mr Vermeer said.

Mrs Vermeer gave her husband a disapproving look. She was very strict about saying unkind things.

"What?" Mr Vermeer said. "It's like a jungle in there."

"Maybe she prefers it that way. It's a nice environment for her kitty cats," Mrs Vermeer suggested.

Mr Vermeer raised his eyebrows and winked at Sienna. He knew his daughter was also a bit suspicious of the goings on next door.

She'd been investigating the perimeter of her neighbour's property. Not snooping, exactly. Just doing some detective work. She was sure Mrs Fitz had a secret, and she was determined to be the one to find out what it was.

Sienna's bedroom window gave her a pretty good view of Mrs Fitz's backyard. It was lonely sometimes, being a nighthawk. Sienna had never been a good sleeper. She was always staying up late to write stories and read and draw pictures. And to practice her detective skills...spying with the binoculars her Opa gave her for her birthday.

The cats would all leave the property as the sun went down, and then return around midnight carrying stuff with their teeth. She recorded it all in a special notebook. Just in case the local police were ever interested.

She came up with a few theories, and shared them over breakfast.

"Her cats are obviously hunting rodents and delivering them to her house, so I think she must have a giant snake in there. Either that or a bunch of owls. Or maybe both! And she's probably training them to attack people. We really need to stay on her good side."

Nolan was getting annoyed.

"Don't be stupid," he said. "You're always ruining stuff with your weird ideas. Where would the rodents even come from? We haven't seen any rats or mice since we moved in. Can't you just be happy about that? Do you even remember waking up with a rat in your blankets on Cedar Street?"

Sienna remembered that infested apartment all too well. Her parents had put these big sticky pads underneath everyone's beds and when they woke up each morning the traps would be covered in centipedes and spiders and sometimes even mice. It was horrible.

Mrs Vermeer's new friend, Tammy, said that none of the houses in town had pests.

"We're just tidy people. Pests don't like tidy, responsible people. And Eerie Creek has a superior waste management system. That's just one reason why this is the best town in the whole world."

Tammy was a talker. She often visited and sat with Mrs Vermeer at the kitchen table for coffee. She worked at the Eerie Creek Chronicle, so she knew everything that was happening around town, and she didn't mind sharing. Sienna liked to listen in.

"By the way," Tammy said one day during March Break, "The Great Chili Cook-Off is coming up in a few weeks. It takes place at town hall each spring as soon as the ice melts off the lake. I've got a sure-fire recipe this year. I can't tell you my secret ingredient, but I'm determined to take the trophy away from old Mrs Fitz. She's won the Best Chili award for the past 25 years. It's a town tradition to try and out-cook her."

When the snow turned hard and crunchy and the days warmed up a bit, Sienna got whiffs that made her mouth water as she passed by her neighbour's iron gate. She realized Mrs Fitz must be making her special chili, and she couldn't wait to try it.

The night before the cook-off, she was woken up by a symphony of screeching cats. She couldn't see anything from her bedroom window, but she was overwhelmed with a pungent smell that she couldn't quite pin down.

In the morning she was exhausted. The school day dragged on. Later, as she walked home, Sienna paused in front of the gate. A white van was parked in the driveway, back doors open. Mrs Fitz was getting ready to deliver her samples to town hall. Just then, something brushed by her leg. A cat! But not an ordinary house cat. As it slinked through the bars, Sienna was horrified by the condition of the feral creature.

She had never seen any of the cats up close before. This one had matted hair, and patches of scratched up skin. Also, something was hanging from its mouth. The cat looked back at her slowly. Its slanted eyes were covered in a pale blue film and its long sharp teeth were pierced into the skin of a...

"RAT! I knew it!"

A long pink twitching tail dangled down. She froze. The cat seemed to twist its mouth into a terrifying smile and tilt its head as if to say, *Follow me! I dare you!*

Sienna was torn. Every bone in her body told her not to investigate, but something weird was happening in that house. And now that she'd seen the mysterious, mangy cat, she was compelled to find out what Mrs Fitz was up to. She hurried home and left a note on the kitchen counter.

Gone to see a friend. If I'm not home by 5 I'll meet you at the Chili Cook-Off.

When she returned to the gate, the cat was still there. Had it been waiting for her? Was this a cry for help? If these cats were being neglected or abused, she would need proof.

Squeezing past a loose post, Sienna followed the cat up the driveway just in time to see it jump into an open basement window. She crept closer and peered inside. The scent of brewing chili was wafting out in fragrant, steamy clouds. And there, almost hidden in the shadows behind a huge, black pot, was a witch-like figure. Stirring, stirring, stirring.

Taking a deep breath, Sienna lowered herself down into the basement. She tiptoed over to a big chest freezer, careful not to make a sound. Her heart was racing. Her body was trembling. And she was loving every second of it. This was the kind of adventure she dreamed about.

She found the perfect spot - hidden, but with a good view of Bobby-Jo and her pot. She would wait for her neighbour to leave for the cook-off, and then search the basement for clues. As she crouched down, she could hear Mrs Fitz grumbling to her cat.

"You didn't see that nosy neighbour girl in yer travels did ya? That little good-for-nothin' peepin' Tom is gonna get what's comin' to her. Curiosity killed the cat!"

The cruel cackle of laughter that followed made Sienna snap out of detective-mode. What was she thinking?! She broke into a crazy cat lady's house and nobody even knew she was there! She had to get out of this evil-smelling dungeon.
She made a move to run toward the window but something was holding her back. Her foot was stuck. Wait…

both feet were stuck! She looked down and saw that she was standing on a giant sticky pad. And she wasn't the only thing stuck there. It was covered in bugs and mice and bloated rats!

She put her hands over her mouth to stop herself from screaming. She was breathing hard and fast and her eyes were bulging with fright! It was the most disgusting thing she had ever seen. She scanned the sticky surface and nearly fainted when she saw that some of the creatures were still wriggling around, struggling to get free... just like her.

If Mrs Fitz discovered her, trapped with the rats, she could only imagine what might happen. She crouched back down and looked around the side of the freezer. The cat she had followed leapt up onto Mrs Fitz's shoulder and dropped his bloody prey into her hand. She stroked his head and gave him a kiss.

Sienna was shocked and horrified as she watched what happened next. Mrs Fitz dropped the dead rat into the boiling pot of Nightmare Chili! Then she muttered to herself as she wiped her hands on a stained apron. "This looks like a juicy one. Ma and Pa would be proud. Those nitwits will pay for how they treated the Fitz family."

Thankfully for Sienna, Mrs Fitz's attention was focused on scooping up spoonfuls of chili and pouring them into little white styrofoam containers. There were stacks and stacks. Enough for the whole town to have a taste. Sienna was feeling sick to her stomach. She couldn't stand the thought of all her friends and family piling rat guts into their mouths. She had to stop it. But how? She was stuck!

As Mrs Fitz started carrying loads of her chili up the stairs to pack into her van, Sienna tried to escape. She wiggled around, but the sticky goo went all the way up to her ankles and she was barely getting anywhere. She slowly managed to squirm her way out of her pants, and then her socks, and then her shoes. It was working! She just had to jump to the edge of the sticky trap!

She used her standing long jump skills to leap over the sea of pasted pests and land on the cement floor just as Mrs Fitz was taking her last load up the stairs. Sienna scrambled up the basement wall and collapsed with relief outside the window. An engine started. Gates creaked open. Mrs Fitz was on her way to the Great Chili Cook-Off with the biggest batch of Nightmare Chili in history.

Sienna made a mad dash for her house. She would warn her family first.

Too late. Nolan had been smelling the chili from next door too, and he was dying to get to town hall before the samples ran out. Mr and Mrs Vermeer were already there, entering their vegetarian chili into the competition.

See ya at the cook-off, Sis, Nolan wrote under Sienna's note. He grabbed his skateboard and left for town just minutes before Sienna barged through the door yelling, "MOM, DAD, NOLAN!!!"

Silence. Nobody was home. She ran outside, jumped on her bike, and pedalled her heart out. She would have plenty of time to stop the madness. It probably took forever to get everything set up. Surely nobody was eating chili yet. But, as she turned the corner toward town hall she could see Mrs Fitz standing beside her van, handing little white containers to hundreds of happy chili-lovers.

She spotted her family. All three of them were sitting at a picnic table. She pumped her legs as hard and fast as she could and started screaming, "STOP! STOP EATING! SPIT IT OUT!!!" She tumbled off her bike as she neared the picnic table. She could see a giant scoop of chili on her mom's spoon and she ran over just in time to slap it out of her hand.

"Sienna! What the heck?! What are you doing? Why aren't you wearing any pants?"

But Sienna couldn't catch her breath enough to speak. She was gasping for air, and as she looked around she realized her rescue mission was hopeless. Nolan's face was covered in bright red chili sauce, and her dad's bowl had been licked clean. Everyone in the "pest-free" town of Eerie Creek was mowing down on rat, mouse, and bug-filled food.

"You *have* to go get a bowl, Sienna," said her brother. "Mrs Fitz's chili is just as amazing as everyone promised. The only thing I didn't like were these tiny onions. I found them a bit chewy, but Mom and Dad thought they were the tastiest part." He tilted his container so Sienna could have a better look. What she saw was no surprise.

A spoonful of gooey little eyeballs stared back at her.

Snowstorm

Winter was their favourite season. That's what brought Jude and Ellie together. They met snowshoeing on a warm spring day, when the woods were silent except for the dripping branches and the birds. They could hear each other's tramping footsteps on the hardened snow for a long time before they crossed on the path.

"Hi," Jude said, confidently.

With wide eyes and nervous laughter, Ellie replied, "Hey, I was hoping you weren't a bear coming out of hibernation. I'm Ellie."

"I'm Jude. Not a bear."

"That's lucky for you. I've got bear spray in my backpack. My mom worries when I go into the woods alone."

"Really? Join the club." Jude pulled a safety whistle out of his coat and blew it."

They soon became best friends, going on adventures together every weekend.

One frigid February day, the sun was bright and there wasn't a cloud in the sky. Jude and Ellie decided to skip school and take the bus up to a trail on the peninsula. They had done this a few times before. They were good students, so their teachers didn't even call home to check up on them.

They made it to the trail, and began forging a new path through the thick woods. They found the edge of the escarpment, and hiked along the cliffs, looking down on icy turquoise waters. When they reached the lookout, they stopped for a bite of granola, sitting quietly on a log overlooking the lake. The sun that warmed them earlier in the day had disappeared, and Ellie zipped her jacket up.

High in the pines, the wind made a lonely kind of sound. A crow cawed at a bluebird. The peace and quiet was a nice change from their noisy classroom. Sometimes they imagined they were the only humans on the planet.

Squeak... squeak... squeak.

They looked at each other with the same thought. In the quiet woods, sounds can be misleading. The growling of a raccoon might have you looking over your shoulder for cougars. Or the high-pitched scream of a red tail hawk might send you running for the hills. But the sound of human footsteps in the snow on a cold day is distinct.

"I really didn't expect to see anybody today," Ellie said.

"Me neither," said Jude. "Maybe the principal is coming to get us."

She laughed.

"But, seriously, are we close to the trail?"

"Not really. It's at least a kilometre to the marked trail where we pick up the loop," he said. "We better get moving. Looks like weather's rolling in."

They packed up their snacks in a hurry and trudged on.

"Moose tracks! And moose scat," Jude said. He was an expert at tracks and bird calls. Ellie was better at identifying trees and plants.

"Mmmmm!" Ellie joked. "Chocolate covered almonds."

"No thanks," said Jude. I'm not THAT hungry. But maybe that's who we heard trekking through the bush back there."

"Could be," Ellie said. But she didn't really believe it.

They were having a great day, even when the wind picked up and a bit of sleet started falling. They didn't mind a winter storm. They stopped to rest, sheltered by the giant roots of a fallen tree. Sleet was turning to snow and they realized it was getting late. They would have to move quickly to catch the bus back to the city.

By the time they reached the meadow, visibility was almost zero. The imprints left by their snowshoes had been blown away. Jude wanted to go in one direction. Ellie wanted to go in another.

"I'm positive! It's this way! Come on!"

When Jude was being stubborn, there was no arguing with

him. Ellie followed reluctantly until they came to the same fallen pine tree where they ate their snack an hour ago. They had just hiked around in a big circle.

"We're lost!" Ellie was mad.

"Okay, then. You take the lead."

Trees were groaning and cracking in the wind as Ellie set off. If she could only see where the sun was, she would be able to follow it west, but the howling storm made that impossible.

She really wished she had packed the compass. Before long, they were in a total whiteout. Jude could barely see Ellie. He was yelling at her to slow down, but they both had their hoods up. The only thing Ellie could hear was her own breath.

When he caught up to her, he grabbed the back of her jacket.

"We have to stick together!" he yelled. "This is getting dangerous!" He pulled some rope out of his backpack and tied it around Ellie's waist. They trekked on through the storm, crouching under branches and climbing over fallen trees. Ellie was relieved every time she felt a tug on the rope to let her know she wasn't alone.

After some tough hiking through the thick bush, they reached a clearing. It looked like an old logging road. Left or right? They had no idea which way to walk so they went left, hoping for the best. Suddenly Ellie halted and Jude bumped into her from behind. Ahead, there was a man standing on the path. It was hard to see him clearly through the blizzard. He stood perfectly still. The wind died down just long enough to notice a large axe slung over his shoulder.

The snowy figure was blocking their way, and Jude and Ellie both had a horrible feeling that he had been pursuing them. Jude pulled Ellie's arm and dragged her into the forest, hoping to escape unseen.

Bushwhacking blindly through the undergrowth, Ellie struggled to keep from panicking. They would never make it back in time for the bus. And it was starting to get dark. The cold was creeping into her bones.

Jude refused to believe they were in trouble. He found another promising trail and took the lead. But they hadn't gone far when the snow-shadowed man blocked the path again!

They changed directions. Over and over. The figure continued to show up, turn after turn. There was no doubt, now, that he was stalking them. Like a hunter.

Ellie's terror gave way to exhaustion. She was losing her willpower. Pushing forward through the strong blizzard winds was sapping her strength. She was so cold and so tired. She sank to her knees.

"I just have to lie down," she yelled to Jude. "Please. Just let me rest for a minute."

"No! Come on! Get up!" Jude was desperate. He knew the danger of falling asleep in the snow.

"You go on ahead. I'll wait here."

Jude scanned the woods. No sign of the man with the axe. He stepped away to check the path ahead.

Ellie took some deep breaths and looked around. To her right, there was a structure, partially hidden by a large rock. A cabin! She tugged on the rope to beckon Jude, but she couldn't feel him there. She pulled in the rope slowly, hand over hand, eventually finding a frayed edge that looked like it had been chopped away.

"JUDE!" She screamed into the whiteout. But there was no point. He would never hear her.

Ellie was alone now. She dragged herself over to the cabin and knocked on the door. It creaked open. She pushed it wider and peeked inside. It was small enough to see that nobody was there. She stumbled in and shoved a chair up against the door handle.

Judging by the old coat hanging over the window, it was a Forest Ranger's cabin. She found a lantern, canned food, firewood and matches. She pushed whatever she could find up against the door before starting a fire, and she thawed out under a wool blanket. She sat quietly, gripping the iron fire poker in case the axe man decided to pay a visit. The smoke coming out the chimney would make it obvious that she was hiding there.

Heavy stomping boots on the cabin stairs let her know that her worst fears were about to be realized.

BANG BANG BANG.

The dresser she placed against the door as a barrier was shaking. She could feel the icy wind as the door opened, inch by inch.

"Let me in! Please! I'm freezing and I'm being followed!"

It was Jude.

Ellie ran to the door and pulled everything aside. She gave Jude a big hug and brought him over to the fire before securing the cabin again.

"Ellie! I saw that scary axe guy and I dove into the woods to hide. The rope broke when I fell hard against a rock. Have a look at my ankle. I think I sprained it."

"Is he gone?"

"No. He practically led me here. Every turn I made, he blocked the path until I saw the cabin."

"It's a trap."

"Maybe. But if he wanted to hurt us, he could have done that back at the lookout." Jude took the big old coat off the hook and wrapped it around both their shoulders.

"I guess we missed the bus," Ellie said. "My mom is going to kill me."

"If the axe man doesn't get us first," Jude joked. But he wasn't laughing. The cabin was pitch black except for the flames dancing in the woodstove. As the wind died down, the friends fell asleep, mentally and physically exhausted.

Morning dawned, cold and clear. Ellie found a park map in the cabin, and navigated them back to the trailhead with ease. There was no sign of the lurker along the way.

With their snowshoes over their shoulders, they walked down the side of the highway warily.

"I'm not really sure I want to go home. We're going to be in so much trouble," Jude said.

"At least we're alive. Do you know how close we were to freezing to death in the storm?"

"I'm trying not to think about that."

At the gas station, they asked permission to use the telephone. Frantic was a good description of Ellie's mother's voice.

"You two stay right where you are. I'll call Jude's mother. She's been awake all night in a panic. Your dad is getting in the car now. He's on his way. And don't think I'm too relieved to get mad. I'm plenty mad! No more adventures for you for a long, long time, young lady!"

"Did you hear that?" Ellie asked Jude.

"Every word!"

The old guy behind the counter was smirking a bit.

"You two get caught in that storm yesterday? She was a wild one! Took me three hours to dig out those gas pumps

34

this morning."

"We were snowshoeing out near the escarpment, and got lost on the far side of the loop. We ended up camping out in an old cabin. Do you know who it might belong to? We need to thank them."

The man looked at the kids curiously.

"There's only one cabin out there. Dicky Harper's old place. He was a Forest Ranger. Best there ever was. Knew every inch of that bush. Spent his days choppin' down trees, and clearin' trails. Poor Dicky."

"What do you mean?" Ellie asked.

"You wouldn't remember that story. It was in all the papers. I suppose it was long before your time. The blizzard of '82. Wicked bad night and a couple of kids got lost. They weren't from around here. Didn't even have a compass on them."

Ellie gave Jude a sheepish look.

"Stubborn old Dicky set out in the snow to find them kids. Somehow they got lucky and turned up over in the Wilson's cow barn. But…"

"Dicky didn't make it?"

"Nope. Must've searched all night long til he took a heart attack by the lookout. Didn't find his body til the spring thaw. His hand was still clutchin' onto that axe of his."

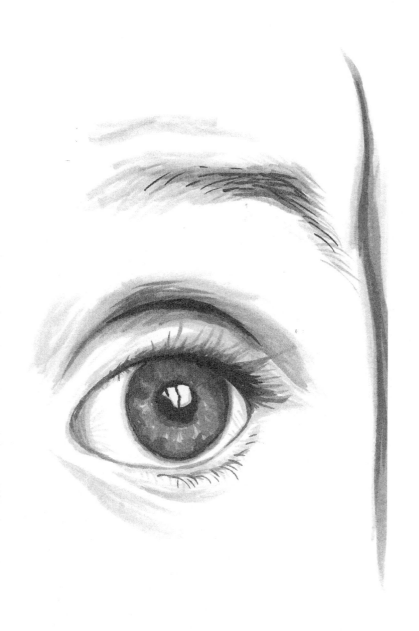

Hangman

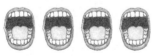

Mr Frook, the English teacher, was the school bully. He stomped the halls in his combat boots, looking for rule breakers. He combed back his long greasy undercut while he tossed around insults. "Nice fedora Joey...not!" When he got angry he punched the lockers with his fingerless gloves. And who knows what was hiding in the pockets of his trench coat?

He was a popular teacher among parents because he'd turned a lot of students around. Especially students who were bad at reading and writing. Grown-ups looked the other way when he was being unprofessional, and they didn't mind that he dressed like a weirdo. Maybe they thought it was cool.

He wasn't very popular with the kids. He was one of those super strict teachers who everyone listened to because it seemed like he could actually lose it. He was passionate about literacy, which was great if you were good at that kind of thing, but it was nerve wracking if you weren't.

When Arlo found out he was going to be in Mr Frook's class, he was pretty upset. Mr Frook didn't let his students participate in school clubs if they were behind in their studies, and the *only* thing Arlo liked about school was the Cross Country Ski Club. He wasn't very good at reading, and his writing was even worse.

On the first day of school, Mr Frook handed out a giant list of really hard spelling words.

"Memorize these by Friday, *or else,*" he said.

The whole class was in hysterics. Everyone was studying during recess and lunch, and Arlo even made his mom quiz him before bed.

When he sat down at his desk on Friday, he was confident about the spelling test. He got every word perfect for the first time in his life, and it felt great. In fact, every kid in the class got every word perfect! It was amazing. Even the ones who didn't usually care about school aced their tests.

This continued into the fall. Arlo and his classmates were becoming excellent spellers, never making a single mistake on a Friday test. In November it finally snowed, and Arlo started his ski practice. It took up a lot of his free time.

After his first week back with the club, he got a word wrong on his spelling test. Not even a word, really. Just one letter. He put *purpendicular* with a 'u' instead of *perpendicular* with an 'e'. Mr Frook flipped out. He smacked a metre stick down on Arlo's desk and kicked a chair across the room. Then in a low voice with his teeth clenched he said, "I'll see you after school."

When the final bell rang, Arlo stayed at his desk, watching the other kids flee for the hills. His buddy Sid gave him a desperate look to say *good luck man, I wish I could help you!*

He held his breath as Mr Frook stared at him in silence.

Eventually his teacher stood up, walked to the board, and drew a little hangman game in the corner.

"Each time you misspell a word on your test, I'll add a body part to the rope. You only get a head, a body, two arms and two legs. None of this hands, feet, and hat stuff."

"How about a bow tie?" joked Arlo.

Mr Frook's eye twitched. No smile.

"Okay… so what happens if you draw the whole body up there?"

"There will be an unthinkable consequence."

And that was that. Arlo left the room confused, but pretty sure that Mr Frook was hinting about the Ski Club. Being taken off the team was the worst consequence he could imagine.

He was juggling everything well for a while, but the spelling words were getting trickier, and the practices were getting longer. He was exhausted. He was falling asleep with his word list beside him, and eventually he got another one wrong. *Handkerchief.* It sure sounded better the way Arlo spelled it, without a 'd'. *Hankerchief.* What kind of a stupid

41

pioneer word was that anyway? Couldn't you just say tissue? Or Kleenex?

Mr Frook drew a little head hanging from the hangman rope.

Arlo was upset with himself, but it was just a head. He had plenty more chances before the "unthinkable consequence" would come his way. After lunch, he noticed that Sid wasn't in class. He asked around, and Shanice told him he went home with a migraine.

The next Friday was no better. He made another spelling mistake. Mr Frook added a body to the hanging head. Arlo was secretly relieved when suddenly, the girl sitting next to him threw up on her desk. Keaton's disgusting puke grabbed everyone's attention. The poor kid was sent home with a bad stomach flu, but Arlo didn't have to deal with the pity from his classmates.

He started to lose his confidence and he decided that he would never be good at spelling. He didn't do much studying that week. When the test rolled around he got two words wrong. He didn't even care that Mr Frook added both legs to the hanging body. He pretended not to notice. He wasn't going to be afraid of his teacher anymore.

During ski practice at lunch that day, he was following close behind his teammate, Smith, who was the fastest skier. Smith whipped around a corner and hit an icy patch. His skis crossed over each other and he tumbled into the bush, screaming in pain.

Arlo raced to his side, but could barely stand to look at his friend's legs. They were twisted and bent in the most unnatural way. There was nothing he could do but run back to school and call for an ambulance.

Monday morning, everyone was whispering about Smith's broken legs on their way into class. When Arlo sat down, he caught a glimpse of the hangman. He gasped. His skin tingled. His thoughts were scrambled. It couldn't be. There's no way. The connection was a total coincidence. Right?

He spent that night going over the events in his mind. The head was drawn, Sid got a headache. The body was drawn, Keaton got a stomach flu. The legs were drawn, Smith broke his legs. If an arm was drawn...would somebody in his class break an arm? What if both arms were drawn? That would be the whole body. He suddenly remembered Mr Frook saying *"Unthinkable consequence"*.

Could somebody die???

The next morning, he met up with Sid and explained his theory on the way to school.

"Are you deranged? It's just a series of ..."

"...weird coincidences? Okay. I know it sounds crazy, but Frook is a freak. I think he might be capable of some kind of paranormal terrorism."

"Look. There's only one way to find out if Frook is actually behind all this," Sid said. "You have to spell another word wrong."

"What?! No way! I'm not gonna break someone's arm. What if I got two words wrong and became a murderer?"

Sid just laughed. "That's not gonna happen. Study hard and just make one mistake. A broken arm isn't that bad anyway. It heals. And besides, you'll feel *way* better when you find out that it's all in your head."

He was right. It was the only way to know for sure.

By Friday morning, Arlo still wasn't convinced that misspelling a word on purpose was a good idea. As it turned out, he managed to get one wrong without even trying.

Nauseous. Come on! He was sure there was a 'c' in that word!

Mr Frook looked genuinely sorrowful as he picked up the chalk and drew an arm on the hangman. Could this lop-sided little stickman mean an injury for someone? Arlo started looking around frantically, scanning the classroom for students in pain. Everyone seemed fine. Maybe Sid was right. His imagination had got the better of him.

On his way out of class, happy to be heading to the cross country trails, Arlo tripped over a trash can and fell on his wrist. It made a sickening snapping sound. A jagged white bone protruded from his bloody wound. It was the worst pain he'd ever felt. He sat there holding his crushed limb, rocking back and forth. Arlo looked at Mr Frook and yelled, "You did this to me! You're hurting everyone! You'll never get away with it!"

Mr Frook calmly notified the office that there was an emergency in room six. Then he knelt beside Arlo with apparent concern and said, "Take deep breaths, Arlo. I wouldn't want you to start feeling *nauseous.*" He raised an eyebrow and smirked.

The paramedics had difficulty subduing Arlo. Everyone stopped and stared as he was wheeled out to the ambulance on a gurney, screaming bloody murder and calling for Mr Frook to be fired. He looked like he was losing his mind.

After surgery, Arlo spent the night in the hospital. His parents heard about his episode at school, and they were worried about him. Why would he yell at his teacher like that? Was he stressed out? Were they pushing him too hard?

They felt so much better when Mr Frook walked into the hospital room to pay them a visit. Arlo was asleep, but his parents had a lovely conversation with his teacher, and thanked him over and over for showing such care and support.

When Arlo woke up, there were flowers on his bedside table with a card. Next week's spelling words were inside, with a note that said,

Study like your life depends on it.

Baby Face

Rebecca and Joel loved thrifting. There wasn't much to do in their town and hardly anywhere to shop for clothes, but there was an awesome thrift store. As siblings, they got along somewhere between okay and not at all. Second Hand Treasures and Delights brought them together. Going there in their parents' busted old sedan was the only thing they liked to do as a team.

It was on one of those trips that, purely by chance, Joel found something special. He spotted it in the toy section - a rubber mask. It was obviously supposed to be a baby. It had a bald head and rosy pink cheeks. Only, whoever made it hadn't done a very good job. It looked more *old man* than *baby*. But Joel saw something else in it right away. Something fun. So he quickly pulled it over his face and searched for his sister.

"Rebecca!" Joel said, standing behind her as she sifted through a rack of denim jackets. Rebecca turned around to see the weirdest, most hideous looking man-baby mask on her stupid brother's head.

"Joel! That's horrible!"

"I know," said Joel, "but doesn't it look just like..."

"Our neighbour, Hank!"

"Exactly."

Hank lived on the farm across from Rebecca and Joel's family. He had a field of corn next to their soybean crops and from time to time they'd see him out there. They never said anything to each other, but Hank always waved.

Hank had a face that had haunted Rebecca since she was a little girl. Her whole family agreed that he wasn't easy on the eyes. But Rebecca found him particularly frightening, because... well, he looked like a baby.

"He's a nice man. He was in a fire as a teenager, that's all," her mom explained. "Be kind."

"No, no," said her dad. "He's a war hero. He saved a bunch of kids by tossing a live grenade out of their schoolyard and it blew up in his face. But your mom's right. There's no reason to be afraid."

Nobody in town had any real proof to back up the rumours about Hank, but that didn't stop them from gossiping.

50

Some people thought he was crazy. Others claimed he was hiding bodies in his cornfields. Rebecca found it hard to sleep at night after hearing each new strange theory. After all, he lived right across the road. Whatever tragedy had happened to Hank, he chose to keep it to himself. So Rebecca kept her distance and respected his privacy.

Joel bought the mask despite Rebecca's pleas to put it back in the costume bin. He also bought a pair of grey denim overalls, a worn plaid shirt and a John Deere cap - an exact replica of what Hank wore every day.

Joel paid, slipped into his newly purchased costume, and chased Rebecca to the car. She got behind the wheel and locked the doors.

"If you want a ride home, you will take that mask off!"

"Me need ride home," Joel said in the creepiest baby voice ever.

She tried to ignore him but he continued to make a scene.

"Waa. Waa. Let me in! Becky mean!"

Joel mashed the baby mask up against her window until she started the car and threatened to abandon him.

"Geez, Rebecca," he complained after he took off the mask and climbed in the passenger side. "You can never take a joke!"

The next morning, Rebecca woke up to find her brother sitting in the chair by her bedroom window in the full Hank costume. John Deere cap, overalls, plaid shirt. Staring eyes peered at her from behind the hideous baby face mask.

"Get out of my room! Get lost forever! You're an absolute nightmare and I hate you," Rebecca said.

Joel just continued to stare, aware that saying nothing,

like Hank would do from across the field, was the scariest tactic.

"Get a life, Loser," Rebecca said, as casually as she could. She grabbed her housecoat and headed down to breakfast, trying not to show her immense discomfort. As cool as she played it, Joel knew he had gotten under his sister's skin, and the game was on.

On the school bus that morning, Joel put the mask on and popped over the backrest of his sister's seat to stare at her until she sensed his presence. When she turned around she was face to face with "Hank". She screamed and everyone looked over, laughing at the ridiculous mask, and at Rebecca for being so frightened by it.

And that's how it went for the rest of the week. On Tuesday, Joel hid in the laundry room and surprised Rebecca with the blank stare of the baby face when she went to fold the towels. On Wednesday, he was waiting for her behind the shower curtain in the bathroom. She was brushing her teeth when the bald head appeared in the mirror and she bit her tongue in terror. Thursday night, he slipped the mask on while Rebecca was engrossed in her favourite TV show. When she turned her head during a commercial, she screamed and spilled her peppermint tea.

"You are such an idiot! I hate you!"

Joel was laughing so hard, he didn't hear the tone of genuine fear in his sister's voice. He was really getting to her. Joel knew the routine was becoming lame, but he found he couldn't stop inventing new ways to scare her.

That Friday, Joel had his best idea yet. He was home early because of a dentist appointment, and couldn't resist a little fun before he got to his weekend chores. When Rebecca

stepped off the school bus, late afternoon shadows were settling over the family farm. She got the eerie feeling she was being watched from across the field.

Sure enough, there was Hank. He raised his hand in a wave. And as always, Rebecca waved back. Only this time, instead of returning to his work, Hank started to walk in her direction. He had never done that before.

Suddenly, as he reached the edge of her family's field, he broke into a run. Rebecca looked over her shoulder at the long curving driveway that led to her house, hoping to find her dad. His tractor was parked in front of the barn, but he was nowhere to be seen. By the time she turned back, Hank was closing in, coming right toward her! Rebecca broke out in a sweat. She froze in place and began to shake uncontrollably. Hank was only a few yards away when she let out a petrified scream.

"Please don't come any closer!"

He stopped just two feet away from her. Then, as she whimpered and peered out from between her fingers, she heard Joel's voice.

"Haha, oh man, that was a good one," he said.

She was stunned, but she managed to choke out the words, "I wish you were dead."

"Oh you'd miss me so much, nerd," said Joel.

Rebecca didn't hear him. Her attention was taken with something over his shoulder and across the field. As Joel turned to see what she was so nervously staring at, he couldn't help but freeze in place too. Quickly, he fumbled to get his mask off and he awkwardly stuffed it into his back pocket.

But it was no use. The figure standing across the field had clearly been watching the whole scene unfold. Dressed in his usual grey overalls and faded plaid shirt, Hank stared at the siblings in silence.

Then, just when Rebecca felt like they couldn't possibly hold their gaze any longer, Hank raised his hand to wave. As Rebecca and Joel waved back, Hank disappeared between the rows of corn.

"Damn," said Joel. "I hope he didn't clue in that I'm doing him."

"Clue in?" cried Rebecca, both terrified and angry. "Doing him? He could obviously tell exactly what was happening. You're so cruel. I wish you would just disappear."

"You're so crazy," said Joel. "He can't see that far with those damaged little eyes. Even if he could, what's he gonna do about it? Tell on us?"

And with that, Joel went inside and made himself a snack.

That night, Rebecca couldn't sleep. She kept thinking about her brother and how unfair it was that he did whatever he wanted without consequences.

That's it, she decided. *I'm going to talk to Mom and Dad. This has gone too far.*

She couldn't stop thinking about Hank. The poor man. Probably self-conscious about his disfigurement and feeling worse because of an insensitive neighbour boy. He must be so lonely.

She decided to wave more enthusiastically and even try to smile the next time she saw him. People thought Hank was a freak, but bullies like her brother were the real freaks.

The next morning, Rebecca rose early to get her chores done. Saturday was her day to clean out the hen house. She got to work, shovelling, scraping, and hosing everything down. Joel had Saturday morning chores too, but he usually slept in. Sometimes Rebecca ended up doing his work for him - not because she wanted to help him out - but because she didn't want her parents to have to do even more than they already did around the farm.

As she walked out to the barn to get some fresh bedding, she was surprised to see that the pigs were already eating happily in their pen. Feeding the animals was one of Joel's jobs. He must've woken up even earlier than Rebecca! Maybe he could sense that she was getting tired of his behaviour. Maybe he was trying to make amends.

She was just about ready to forgive him when she opened the big barn door and her heart jumped into her throat. She spotted the baby faced figure in the shadows, rinsing out slop pails. But she recovered quickly this time. Doing chores in his costume? Joel had taken his joke too far.

"As if you didn't learn your lesson yesterday," Rebecca said.

Joel stayed quiet and continued to stare. It didn't matter how many times her brother did it. That mask didn't get any less creepy. It was so realistic.

"I wish you weren't my brother," said Rebecca.

Suddenly she was overwhelmed with a new feeling of uneasiness. As her eyes adjusted to the shadows, her gaze drifted down to see a pair of workboots much larger than Joel's.

The overalls were dirtier than Joel's.

The eyes were blacker than Joel's.

"Ain't yer brother," the scratchy voice said. "Don't be worryin' 'bout him no more."

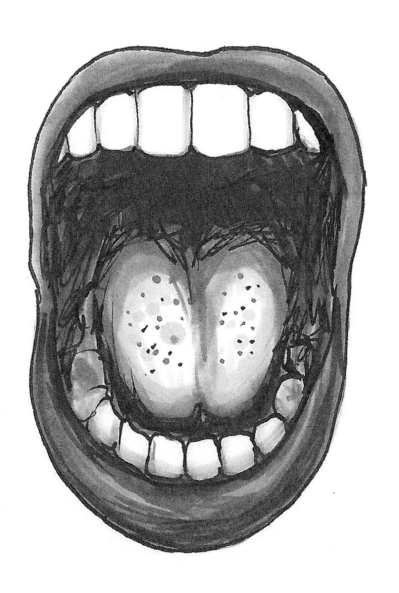

WARNING:

SIX SCREAM STORY AHEAD

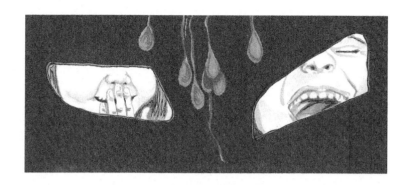

Pumpkin Head

Peter was one of those shy, quiet kids who could blend into the wall on a dreary day. But when the clouds parted and the sun shone down, his brilliant orange hair could blind a person. It was beautiful. But of course, as a kid in Grade 6, it was *different* and so it caused him a lot of grief. He was an easy target for the classroom bullies. They tried out all kinds of nicknames, and the one that stuck was Pumpkin Head.

Peter did his best to ignore the teasing. He knew his parents were right, and the kids at school were just insecure. But it still hurt sometimes. He daydreamed about getting revenge. Especially on Donald - the meanest boy who always had a crowd of followers around him.

Peter would spend his evenings up in his bedroom, building little figurines out of modelling clay and plotting ways to teach Donald a lesson. Of course, he would never actually go through with any of it. He was a peaceful child. Sensitive to people's feelings.

As Halloween drew nearer, the name-calling got worse. Maybe all the kids had pumpkins on their minds. When none of the teachers were around, Donald would sing *"Pumpkin Head, Pumpkin Head, we'll scrape out your guts until you're dead."* Even when teachers were close, he would hum the tune and act all innocent.

Peter had to practice self control. He took deep breaths and repeated different things to himself, like, *Don't show a reaction. Don't give them what they want. They're weak. They're childish. You're better than them.*

In mid-October Peter's class was having a pumpkin carving competition. He was excited because he was good at sculpting with clay and he was pretty sure he could make a wicked jack-o'-lantern. He really wanted to win first prize, a giant jar of jelly beans.

But Donald had other plans for the day. He brought in his own pumpkin that he had picked specially from Lindley's Farm. He had already sawed a big hole in the top, scraped out the inside, and carved a creepy face into it. When he brought it to school he was showered with compliments.

One of his followers said, "Whoa, cool pumpkin Donald. But why's it upside down?"

"Just wait and see," he said with a suspicious grin.

When the bell rang, Donald hauled his upside down pumpkin into class and suddenly Peter felt something slimy get pushed onto his head and over his face. He could barely breathe through the jagged, carved mouth and his vision was blurred behind the slanted eye holes. He was shocked. Terrified. It took him a moment to realize what was happening. He had a pumpkin on his head!

His classmates started laughing hysterically and pointing as he struggled to pull it off. It was wedged on tight and totally stuck! Panic set in and he ran for the door, bumping into desks and chairs in his path. He sprinted down the hall, past the screeching sounds of joy and amusement. He was losing his breath when he stumbled into the principal who rushed him to her office to remove the pumpkin.

She sat him down and yanked as hard as she could, but it didn't budge.

"Hey Mr Chen, get in here," she yelled to the vice principal.

Mr. Chen came over, put a knee on Peter's shoulder and pulled up on the pumpkin with all of his strength. Peter was moaning in pain. It wasn't working.

"We're going to have to cut it off," Mr Chen suggested.

"It's too risky. We might cut his head! We'd better call an ambulance and get him to Emerg."

Next thing Peter knew, he was sitting in a hospital room, getting the pumpkin sawed off his head with a cast cutter. Pieces of orange gourd fell to the floor, sticky and slimy. Peter gasped for fresh air and broke into tears. He collapsed into his mother's arms.

Nothing his parents could say seemed to calm Peter down. Bad dreams kept him awake all night. After a week of horrible nightmares, the entire family was so exhausted that work and school were out of the question. There was only one solution. They would have to sell their house and move away.

Back at school, Donald wasn't getting the praise and recognition he expected. Once the other kids realized how upsetting the whole event was for Peter - upsetting enough to leave town - they felt awful. They wished they had helped him instead of standing by, laughing. Donald didn't get it.

"What kind of wimp can't handle a little teasing?" he said.

The principal called Donald's dad to have a conversation

about bullying. He scoffed at her concerns. In fact, Donald's dad bragged about his son's behaviour.

"My tough little guy. He's just showin' the other kids who's boss. I never let anybody push me around, and you know what they say, the apple doesn't fall far from the tree."

"Indeed," the principal concurred.

Within days, parents in the community made it clear that Donald was not welcome in their homes. The gang who used to follow him around found nicer friends. By Halloween, no one was allowed to trick-or-treat with him.

Who cares, he thought. *I'll just go by myself.*

So he put a goblin mask on under his hoodie and headed out with a pillowcase in hand. He wanted to hit the rich blocks first, which were just past Peter's old house. He spotted the SOLD sign as he walked by and could see through the windows that the place was empty. No furniture, no pictures on the walls, and no car in the driveway.

"See ya later, sucker," he said under his breath.

Then he heard a tapping noise. It sounded like it was coming from inside the house. Donald turned and slowly looked up to see the silhouette of a pumpkin in the upstairs window. Tap. Tap, tap, tap. Donald jumped back a little, and then laughed.

What a weirdo, he thought. *I bet he left that pumpkin up there to scare me.*

Up and down the leaf-littered streets, Donald couldn't shake the feeling that he was being followed. Laughing groups of ghosts and skeletons passed him by. Little witches crossed the street to avoid him.

He was alone. But a shadowy presence seemed to linger behind him, just out of sight. He tried to act brave, but he kept looking over his shoulder. He was catching glimpses of pumpkins in all the windows now. Was that a pumpkin-headed scarecrow in the darkened alley? Every jack-o'-lantern he saw had the same jagged smile and slanted eyes he had carved into Peter's pumpkin.

His pillowcase was only half full when he panicked and ran back toward his house. Even with his warmest jacket, he was shivering. He wanted to lock all of the doors and hide under the covers.

With great relief, he crossed the street onto his own block. He took a deep breath. Safe! Home never looked so good. Until... what? Someone, or something was on his front porch. He stopped and stared. It was a dummy, stuffed with leaves, propped in a chair, with a pumpkin for a head.

All his life, Donald had been a master at hiding his emotions.

Scared? Act tough.

Worried? Act mean.

Sad? Act like you don't care.

But his nerves got the better of him and he yelled at the top of his lungs.

"WHAT DO YOU WANT?"

Nothing. Not a sound or a movement.

"I'm not afraid of you," he said, barely able to disguise the trembling fear in his voice.

He climbed up onto the porch, one step at a time. As he went for the door knob he heard a loud "ARGHH!" Two big hands reached out and grabbed him from behind. He screamed and kicked and flailed his arms until he noticed the dummy laughing and taking the pumpkin head off. It was his dad. Of course it was his dad. He was always pulling this kind of thing. He thought he was being hilarious but he was really just being a jerk.

"What a baby! Baby Donald! Did I raise a coward?" his dad teased. "You were so scared! You were screaming like a little girl! I hope you don't wet the bed tonight."

Donald stormed inside and up to his room. He was furious.

He dumped out his pillowcase. What a bad night. A bunch of apples, some homemade fudge that was probably poisoned, and a handful of the smallest chocolate bars in the world. He opened a tiny box of Smarties. Six. Six Smarties. The worst Halloween ever.

Or was it? Donald ate the Smarties, crunching them in one mouthful.

He wondered about his classmates, and how much fun they were having running from street to street together in the dark. He never wanted to spend another Halloween trick-or-treating alone. He unwrapped a toffee and it got stuck in his teeth. All month he had been anticipating the fun of this night and he was miserable.

"Even Peter probably had a better Halloween than I did," he said, digging around in his limp pillowcase.

Knock, knock, knock.

Donald did not want to talk to his father. He pulled the sheets over his head. The door opened a crack.

"Is the little sucky baby going to bed early? Does he need a bottle? Did he put his diaper on? Well, nighty night, then!" The door closed and Donald pushed his face into his pillow to stop the tears from flowing.

I never wanna be like him, he thought. *He's the worst kind of person. I should run away.*

But, where would he go? Who would go with him? Nobody, that's who. He had zero friends. Lonely was a new feeling for Donald. It was no fun to trick-or-treat alone. It was no fun to wander around the schoolyard at recess without buddies. What had gone wrong?

And then, as the full moon peered through his window, he realized something. He was *exactly* like his dad. He was just as cruel. Just as thoughtless. No wonder the kids at school didn't want to hang out with him anymore.

He dug around in the bottom of his pillowcase for a candy to comfort him. Instead he pulled out a little clay jack-o'-lantern. It was well-carved and painted bright orange. Donald pulled the stem, expecting a candy to be inside. Instead, he found a tiny piece of paper. A gift certificate maybe? Cool.

He unfolded the note and read a familiar rhyme.

Pumpkin Head, Pumpkin Head, we'll scrape out your guts until you're dead!

Donald bolted upright and looked around his room. Every shadow seemed to hide fearful possibilities. Someone wanted to teach him a lesson. Well, it was working! Next Halloween, he vowed, things will be different. Just because my dad's a bully, doesn't mean I have to be one. I can change. It can't be that hard to be nice. I might even find out where Pumpkin Head, I mean Peter, is living and send him a letter to apologize.

He really was sorry. Sorry for missing out on a fun Halloween. Sorry for having such a terrible dad. Sorry for himself.

The next morning Donald woke up to a bright sun shining through the window. The cobwebs of fear had been wiped clean. This was day one of a new, better, kinder Donald. How hard could it be to act nice? Fake it 'til you make it, Mr Chen always said.

He stretched and walked into the bathroom. His mouth was feeling fuzzy. Too many candies before bed. He reached for his toothbrush and squirted a big gob of toothpaste onto it. His lips were stiff and kind of numb. Weird.

As he pushed the toothbrush into his mouth, a tooth fell out. Hadn't he lost all his baby teeth? Wow, just another thing for his dad to bully him about. *Baby still losing baby teeth?* Breakfast would be unbearable. Donald pulled the brush out of his mouth. Out came a bunch of teeth. They clattered into the sink. What?! Wait! Those weren't teeth in the sink. They were pumpkin seeds.

Donald looked in the mirror. Slanted eyes and a jagged smile glared back at him. He screamed and jumped away. The pumpkin head jumped away too. He leaned in, and the pumpkin head leaned in.

He grabbed the ghoulish gourd with both hands and tried to pull it off. But it was firmly attached to his shoulders. He gasped at his creepy reflection and punched the mirror hard enough to smash it to pieces. Stringy orange pumpkin guts oozed out of the fresh cuts in his hand.

Echoing inside his hollow head was a humming noise. He tried to cover his ears, but he had no ears. Nothing could quiet the horrible taunting.

"*La, la, la,*
La, la, la,
we'll scrape out your guts
until you're dead."

And now for a TRUE story...

...it happened to a friend of a friend of ours...

The Back Seat

It was a long, slow drive through hill country to get to Jonah's dad's house. He made the trip every other weekend. The villages along the way had strange names. Crooked Hollow. Foggy Town. Eerie Creek. He liked watching the rundown homesteads go by. There was something comforting about the old folks sitting on sloping porches and the crumbling cabins sinking into overgrown fields.

Jonah wasn't one of those kids who kept asking "Are we there yet?" He was perfectly happy daydreaming about the big families that lived along these lonely lanes a hundred years ago. He imagined fireside stories and a granddad who played the fiddle, and a houseful of brothers and sisters.

Jonah's mom invented a game to make the drives more interesting. They called it Random Route, choosing different backroads and highways each time they drove to Greenville, always hoping to discover a faster way. They were determined to beat their best time of 2 hours and 27 minutes, but it usually took closer to 3.

Jonah gave his dad a quick call to say they were leaving, before unfolding the map. He was the navigator.

"So where should we stop for supper this time?" asked his mom. "Super Burger or Champ Burger."

"Actually, I found a new route that avoids Highway 10 altogether. It looks like a short cut. There might not be any fast food places."

"Oooh sounds promising. Maybe we'll find an old-fashioned diner. Where to?"

"Take Sideroad 5 to Wallowing Way, and then left on Lost Mile Road. It looks like it'll take us most of the way to Dad's."

Jonah's mom raised an eyebrow. "I've never heard of that road. Random Route, here we go. Start the timer, Jonah!"

At first, everything on Lost Mile Road looked pretty normal. Vegetable stands, quaint shops, and rolling hills. They almost pulled into a Chip Truck that advertised a bucket of fries for eight dollars, but decided to wait. Bad idea. The landscape changed and they hit some bumpy gravel.

"Wow, you've really led us on an adventure this time," Jonah's mom joked.

Tall wildflowers lined the ditches and golden corn fields went on forever. No buildings in sight. It was a peaceful drive. They both enjoyed the quiet of their own thoughts.

"Hmm," Jonah's mom said, breaking the silence.

"What?"

"The compass. We were heading west for the longest time and then it said south, then east, and now it's gone."

"Gone?"

"Yeah. Look at the dashboard. The top right hand corner where the compass usually is. It's blank."

Jonah reached forward and pressed the information button.

"Anything now?"

"Nothing. I hope the electronics aren't screwing up. I really can't afford to get this car fixed again."

Outside, the wind picked up. The weeds in the ditches went flat. A branch broke off a tree and skittered across the road in front of them. "Green clouds," said Jonah. "Isn't that the sign of a tornado?"

"It can be," said his mom. "But they weren't calling for extreme weather today. I'm sure we're very safe." She changed the radio station to catch the local report.

Heavy rain came out of nowhere and pounded against the windshield, quickly turning to hail. Golf balls were crashing against the car and Jonah was in awe. "Holy! I've never seen hail like this before!"

His mom was finding it hard to see. She adjusted her rearview mirror and squinted. All of a sudden she screamed and jumped in her seat!

"What happened?" yelled Jonah. "Are you okay?"

"Oh... oh sure," she replied, catching her breath. She looked like she'd seen a ghost. "I... I thought I saw... something in the back seat."

Jonah turned to look over his shoulder, but there wasn't anything there. "What did you see?"

"It must've been a reflection. Nothing to worry about."

Jonah laughed nervously. "Okay...should I be concerned about you Mom? I mean I know you're getting old... but seeing things too? Maybe I should drive the rest of the way." She rolled her eyes and chuckled. Jonah was years away from getting his license. They both relaxed a bit, but the storm continued, and Jonah's mom had to concentrate hard on the road ahead.

The clouds thickened and soon the landscape was completely black. All that could be seen was a small section of gravel in front of the car.

"Reach over into the back seat and get my sweater, will you, Jonah? I've got a chill." As he unfastened his seatbelt, the voice on the radio crackled. It was replaced by haunting, high-pitched music. Jonah tried turning the dial, but it was stuck. He grumbled to his mom, "Are we seriously gonna have to listen to this creepy opera lady for the rest of the drive?" She didn't answer. "Mom?" All he could hear was the pattering hail on the rooftop. "Mom!"

It was so dark inside the car that he couldn't even see her face. Just her breath, coming out in small, icy clouds.

"Geez! It's freezing! Let me get your sweater." The heat didn't seem to be working at all. He began to shiver too. But as he shifted in his seat to reach back, he had an overwhelming

76

notion that he should NOT move. Someone was there. Right behind him. In the back seat. He was never as sure about anything in his entire life. All his senses told him to FREEZE.

Suddenly the headlights went out. Then the dashboard lights. Darkness. The opera turned off and the hail stopped. Silence.

"Mom," Jonah whispered. No answer. He couldn't see a single thing. He wasn't even sure he was still in the car. He felt totally alone like a planet floating far out in the galaxy.

"Mom," a little bit louder this time. Nothing.

Jonah's breath was coming in small, panicky gulps. He forced himself to breath in and breath out. Why on earth did he think that Lost Mile Road was a good choice? He would give anything to see the brightly lit Champ Burger sign right now.

"MOM!"

Three things happened all at once. The lights came back on. The car approached a curve. And Jonah's mom stepped on the gas.

"SLOW DOWN!"

She hit the brakes. The tires skidded on the gravel and came dangerously close to the ditch, but the car miraculously swerved along the soft shoulder and got back on track.

"Wow. Sorry. That curve came out of nowhere! You okay, Jonah?"

Jonah croaked out a moan. "Not sure," he managed to say.

"So... can you get my sweater now?"

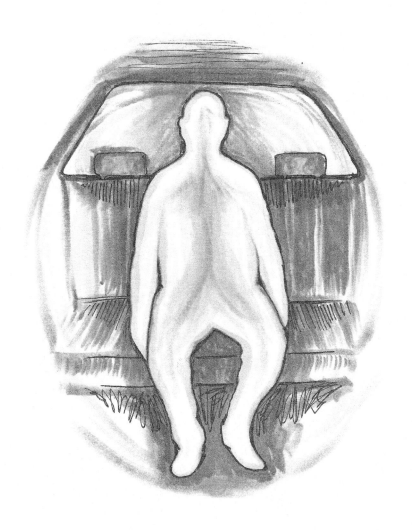

The storm had cleared and the moon was peeking out from behind the clouds. Feeling cautious, Jonah turned his head to look at his mom. She seemed totally normal. He looked over the back seat. Nothing there but his backpack and his mom's sweater. He snatched it, half expecting something to grab his arm. But nobody was behind him.

What the heck just happened?! Jonah knew his imagination was too vivid sometimes, but he couldn't have imagined all that... could he have? The total blackout? His mom being frozen? Or did she disappear? Or what?! It was worse than a nightmare. Or WAS it a nightmare? Could he have fallen asleep?

Civilization had never looked better. Streetlights! People! Stores!

"I'm starving," Jonah's mom said as she screeched off the road. Jonah realized that he was intensely hungry too. They shared the best pizza they had ever tasted. On a full stomach, Jonah's heartbeat slowed down. The evil backseat passenger and the strange dark journey were just dreams. Simple. He nodded off. His mom didn't mention anything unusual about the trip, so he didn't either. *Forget it*, he told himself, and as they turned the corner onto his dad's street, he felt calm and safe.

"Hey, did you take a look at the time, Jonah? How did we do today? It seemed pretty quick," his mom said.

Jonah picked up her phone from the compartment between the seats to check the stopwatch. "Your phone's dead, Mom."

"Really? No way. I had it plugged in all day."

Jonah fiddled with it but nothing happened. "It's definitely dead."

"Uh oh," she said. "Looks like a police cruiser in front of your dad's house. I hope everything's okay." They pulled into the driveway.

When Jonah's dad opened the front door he looked pale and concerned, and then he grabbed Jonah and hugged him harder than he'd ever hugged him before.

"Where have you two been?!" he asked with urgency. "Why weren't you answering your phone? These police officers checked your apartment and there's an APB out on your car."

"Calm down, Doug," Jonah's mom said. "We left home about three hours ago. Maybe less. We took a shortcut. Well, that storm might've slowed us down a bit, eh Jonah?"

"What are you talking about? A storm?"

"You didn't get all that hail down here? You should've seen the size of the…"

"Rachel!" Doug jumped in. "It's Sunday night. You guys have been missing for two days."

The police officers looked at them curiously. They were staring accusingly at Jonah's mom.

Jonah's dad bent down and looked him in the eyes. "Are you okay, Son?" he asked.

"Yeah. I'm fine! We just took a new route, that's all," Jonah said. "Let me get the map from the car and show you."

The map was creased and worn from so many trips. Jonah unfolded it on the dining room table and several pairs of questioning eyes looked over his shoulder. He pointed to their route with a shaking finger. He was having trouble finding it.

"Lost Mile Road…" he said. "I swear it was right around here…"

THE END

You're a brave soul. But are you brave enough for the next book?

Follow us on Instagram and check out our website:

@spookystuffbook
www.spookystuffbook.com

- Find out more about our upcoming volumes

- Learn how to make your drawings look creepy

- Take a spooky photo while reading this book, and tag us for a chance to win a terrifying prize!

About the Authors

Jon and Di Nelson are totally normal, not at all creepy, strangely average people. They live in Owen Sound, Ontario, in a house that is not haunted (as far as they know). They have two beautiful monster children who wreak havoc on their otherwise peaceful lives.

They have fond childhood memories of being frozen stiff in their bunks on hot summer nights, listening to frightening stories at overnight camp. And they still love canoe trips and bonfires, storytelling and spooky stuff.

Printed in Great Britain
by Amazon

67723193R00058